This is a work of fiction. Names, characters, places, and incidents are either the product of the author's imagination or used fictitiously, and any resemblance to actual persons, living or dead, business establishments, events or locales is entirely coincidental.

CYBERPUNK XXX-ROTIC

All rights reserved.
Copyright © 2024 By Mikhail McCann

This book may not be reproduced in whole or part, by scanning or any other means, without permission. Making or distributing copies is prohibited.

CYBERPUNK xXx-ROTIC

CARTER HOLLAND

Dedicated to hardcore cyberpunk

VISIT ME ONLINE For Carter Holland news on book releases and join the newsletter at

https://cybernexus2088.systeme.io

Table of Contents

1. Painful Lust Vers~4.0

2. Hell fucked right up the ass!

3. Never back down, Bitch!

4. Penetrated up her ass, you say?

5. It's all fun and games until some muthafuck ruins your 200 thread shirt!

6. Get that fucker by the balls!

7. (Chinese accent) Yeah, Fuck your sister! Middle finger in the air.

8. Wetworks

1 Painful Lust Version~4.0

///Entry: -Give it to me raw. Ya big hunk of a man. Thrust me you fucking animal.-Molly XXX

///Entry: -I have to warn you it will hurt and no amount of pain can be withstood by me.-Devermando

---

She feels wholesome thickness filling her tight hole, screaming and almost shedding tears of pain. The cum explodes inside of her.

She looks behind and sees his cock throb of semen juices all over it.

The mark of his handprints are on her pale creamy butt, she loves those cybernetic black hands on her.

The sheer raw power of them. She leans herself back up from the doggy style position turning around.

Her pink hand grabs his small dark fleshy mushroom tip slowly moving down to the girthy metal chrome cock that is as long as her forearm.

She smiles with her bright neon green teeth showing and the light from outside the building shines through the half closed blinds.

The sound of fast cars zip by in the Island nation of Cyber Bang City. Riding the highways surrounding the city.

It's loud and roaring with sexual life.

"Oh, Molly. You feel so good inside. Nice and warm."

Molly XXX screams while straddling his massive chrome cock. Making uncontrollable facial expressions while holding her ass with both hands moving up and down.

Smashing her vagina down the shaft and she pounds the shit outta of Devermando.

He rolls his eyes back leaning back over the edge of the mattress with his arms over his head.

Molly XXX keeps going and can't stop coming from ecstasy and fiery lust inside her soul.

"God fucking damn, you are amazing!"

She pulls off him fast still shuddering and Molly XXX starts squirting juices all over his hard chiseled chest.

The liquid flows down his neck and face and he takes a taste of it in his full mouth.

Swallowing it down his throat.

He pulls her off him, placing her face down on the mattress using his black cybernetic hands, turning her over with her ass up in the air and he sticks it in her juicy hole that is still squirting out. "I'm not done with you, slutty b+tch," he said with a rough growly voice.

Devermando is pile-driving her with his foot on her face and she feels him pounding her juices back inside her pink beat pussy and he pulls out once or twice letting her squirt out down her legs.

She grabs onto the mattresses red colored bed sheets.

Molly XXX moans so loudly. That Cyberpunkie patrons hear her getting fucked through the thin yellow shit stained walls.

The hallway is narrow and multiple flashlights from down the stairs begin to move up the shitty yellow walls, black cyber-guns of modified AR-15's placed in the hands of bad mercenaries in dark armored suits run through the halls.

One of them sees the couple fucking through thermal imaging goggles around his eyes.

The helmet. A one piece skull formed mask and black straps behind her long blond hair.

Shaggy and dirty like she hasn't cleaned herself up in two days.

She hears two people coming, two Cyberpunkie alpha males appear from the other end of the hall.

The Mercenary does a hold position to the other mercs. And they stop waiting.

A pistol pulls out of her side and she waits to see if they see them. They do and immediately put their hands up. She fires at them. Dead.

"Fucking faggots."

(P.S. Don't get triggered - The Author)

Back to the couple in the room and they stop fucking for a minute. Getting off the bed.

"What was that?" Molly XXX whispers.

"Not sure. Get your shit and grab the weapons," Devermando said.

Molly XXX and Devermando hit it up fast putting their cybernetic latex armored suits on.

While stocking up on weapons and grenades along with some cyber blades.

Devermando has an incendiary grenade in hand flicking the pin out.

"You ready, babe?" he said.

"One...
...two!" she yelled out.

The black incendiary grenade goes BOOM!, in the hallway.

2. Hell fucked right up the ass!

"Fuck you muthafucka's!" Molly XXX screaming. Her blood boiled of violent outbursts.

She sees the Mercenary squad of killers trying to dodge the hail of incandescent bullets exploding through the walls.

A few Cyberpunkie patrons in the rooms dodge the exploding bullets.

Some of them get hurt, others don't even notice it while tripping out on Nano-cid in cyberspace.

High as fucking shit with a grin on their face. Ready to die in a heart pounding minute.

Her double SMGS click rapidly from her fingers on the trigger. Full empty mags depleted.

"Shit fuck I'm out, love. My vag is all hot and heavy for more."

Devermando pops out seeing the mercenaries and the Blonde hot babe in red sneak away in between the walls behind them.

Just saving her big bubbly bare naked ass chaps showing from the onslaught incoming.

"We are fucking here to take you out for the crime against the Empires edgerunners!" she yelled out from behind the many Mercs.

"Those Edgelords got what they deserved for exterminating my Bloodhounds. Cunt!" He screamed.

-Edgelords, psycho special forces of Einhander S.E.V wars that fought the nano-mutated Hunter Killers prior to this story. Battle B included.-

"There's no way out of here, muthafuck," the Blonde babe said.

Devermando opens fire by pressing on the trigger of his modded mini-gun that has customized neon barrels and red hot spikes that fire out of steel. Five inches long tubes through the body and explodes the internal organs.

Two Mercs take hits from the red spikes, one through the codpiece hitting his hard cock inside straight into the pelvis and the other takes one in the neck under the metal white skull helmet.

Her eyes react to the hit and she feels the spike begin to vibrate with the sound of her screaming voice.

"Ahhhhhhh!"

The head explodes in violent gory pieces of blood shooting up the walls and outward at the Mercs behind her.

Her brain splatters on their guns and forearms as they flick it off.

"Holy fuck shit, that's gross!"

The other is still reeling from the groin pain and opens fire on the Death-Heads and they see him.

"Incoming!" Molly XXX yelled, shoving her lover into the door crashing into the next room.

They both see the codpiece and long black cock flying past the door frame with blood shooting like a bucket of water onto the ground in front of the entrance.

"Fuck that was a fucking close one," Devermando said holding onto her tits cupping them and he feels her hand around his thick cock.

"Guess we are like minded sickos," she said laughing.

3. Never back down Bitch!

The Merc squad moves on up across the hall next to the door frame and they stop.

The Blonde Merc breathes heavily through her mask.

She nods at the Merc to check on them.

One of them uses his white trimmed infrared goggles to enhance his eyes through the piss stained walls searching for the Killer couple known as the Death-Heads.

"No sign of them in the room. They must have escaped fate."

"I call bullshit," Merc one said.

"Yeah, I second that," Merc three said.

-The blonde bangs her head like fuck it in her mind. I'm with some hot horny stupid fucks and I could take them all on in a gangbang of my fucking dreams, she thought to herself feeling all wet and juices flowing out of her loose beat meat vagina. Ah fuck it, it's never gonna happen.-

"What do you mean you can't fucking find them dick-less shit?!" she yelled at him.

The Mercs stare at each other with fear from the Blonde. "Filthy mouth much, Kenzie-Ho?"

"It's enough I gotta deal with a bitch like you leading men like us. Maybe I should just fuck you up right in the ass," Merc three said.

"You would like that, would cha. Ya pretty boy Jap?"

"Fuck you racist cunt," he said.

"You lucked out, getting hired as a former Yakuza bitch toy like yourself with mommy issues."

He ignores her and the sound of feet scurrying away elevates their inhibitors as two rats pass 'em from wall hole to wall hole.

They hear running sounds coming at them, it's too late as a blade hits Merc two internally in the side ribs hitting his kidney and pulls out fast.

The sudden terror in his eyes goes into shock and death hitting the ground floor hard.

Kenzie-Ho sees nothing in a frenetic panic blasting her modded Sammy shotgun with hollow bullets into the walls creating massive holes in them.

"Fuck, where the hell's ya at bitches!"

She steps on the two faggots cocks squashing the crotches to fleshy bits and blood squirts out around her black boots.

The right boot smashes one of the faces too without noticing.

-Eyeballs pop out of the socket of the golden skinned dead faggot. Possibly of Islander descent. Ancient Chamorro perhaps, she thought.-

Kenzie-Ho moves on up a few more steps and suddenly a SWISH! sound hits her thigh—- she goes down hurt.

Her eyes widened seeing an invisible predator with a katana and its big cock exposed flopping back and forth heading straight for the others.

She lays down feeling nauseated with a feeling of wanting to vomit but she breathes it in slowly seeing the bare ass of the new killer coming into play.

-*What's his story? A private contract killer or something else. Is he fucking in it for the money or just pure revenge.*-

She feels a tug of her leg being grabbed and looks up at Devermando taking her into the elevator and Molly XXX pushes the button.

They hear screams of the other Mercs being killed in action by the new killer.

The door closes and they see the katana blade in hot pink saber form through the steel door.

Devermando fires his hand cannon from his hip holster, aiming out at the steel elevator doors.

The katana saber pulls away and silence.

The Blonde Merc has her side arm aimed at the couple and they suddenly see her with a reaction too.

"The fuck did you save me for?" she asked.

Molly XXX spreads her legs out showing off her latex suit with her ass cheeks spread out in front of Devermando behind her. His arm is right over her shoulder with his hand cannon.

"We got a job for you along with the sexual offer too," she said.

Kenzie-Ho raises her eyebrow at them and smiles.

"There better be one hot fucking threesome in it for me."

4. Penetrated up her ass,you say?

The digital numbers increase by each floor as they watch it go up.

14...,16...,19...

The elevator sound dings on the 21st digital number on the panel within the seedy hotel opening the steel doors slowly revealing a loud sound of hard banging strobe lights hitting their eyes.

The place is a fucking maze compared to the hallway that they got fucked up in.

Nothing, but a bunch cyberpunkies in a trance of LSD coma wearing various neon colored visors across their faces and the crew walk through the crowd entering the maze of hardstyle trance music blasting in their ears.

"This place will provide us some good cover for a while," Devermando said.

"Well, in that case let's make the most fun out of it," Molly XXX said to them.

Kenzie-Ho moves in on Molly XXX unzipping her latex suit revealing her tits and they both start moving into a black small six hundred square foot room with a queen size elevated bed.

Devermando watches as he sits on a floating chair seeing them make love of finger banging, tit sucking as he strokes his long fat cock up and down slowly with his black cybernetic hand. Cum seeps out a bit. But he holds it in until he gets in on the action with them.

-Women you gotta fucking love the touch of their skin and feel of the meat flesh inside their soul.-

-Molly XXX sees him in the chair thinking about all the nasty things she wants him to do. Maybe a double penetration on the new babe they acquired. She wouldn't mind a slap across the face too. She loves that shit.-

"Come to us, you delicious fucking bad man and play with our hot juicy cunts."

Molly XXX summons him to the bed with her finger doing a come over here now motion.

Kenzie-Ho skin in the strobe lit area is so smooth looking, young and her ass. Man that ass is a big plushy white tush.

Devermando stiffens and hits against her booty, slapping his cock against her jiggly white butt. She laughs touching his hard pecs. "My those things are hard as fuck just like your fat cock I want inside my anus," she said.

She is sticking her finger in her mouth pulling saliva out of her mouth's lush pink lips. Spreading her spit around Devermando's long fat cock holding it and leading it to her anus.

-Finally a man in my anus fucking like the sinners of Cyber Bang City. The pain of being fucked by the immense size spreads my hole even bigger and I love every fucking hard bang a minute. I scream of sounds so uncontrollable that I shudder when his beautiful cock comes inside me multiple times. I roll my eyes back falling into Molly XXX pussy, eating her out.-

The music goes on for another fifteen minutes and they hear gunfire erupt in the maze of the private room.

Blood splashes across them as they see black masked figures pass them with MP7 semi-automatics and purple saber steel swords.

One of the Ninja's slides down on the floor slicing a blonde big titted bimbo through the waist. Cutting her body in half.

"Fucking Ninja X Fuckers!"

"Get your shit, time to fight these fuckheads and survive what's next," Molly XXX said.

Kenzie-Ho cranks her SMG back and leaves her helmet and half her armor suit behind with just her beautiful white tits and pink nipples exposed.

"I'm ready to fuck 'em up, you two babes ready to do more after this?"

The Death-Heads laugh and head out with gunfire hitting the walls and scream at the Ninja X Fuckers. A head slice or two across the floor and heads are still rolling.

5. It's all fun and games until some muthafuck ruins your 220 thread shirt!

The enemy that is as large as a giraffe takes big steps up the stairs in a black trench coat wearing red armor under it.

That goes up to his neck line. The red beast with a personal weapon pounding destruction between its legs moves silent through carpeted blood soaked bodies of the Mercs and sniffs the air.

It knows something is here. It can smell the fragrance of a young but lethal assassin.

Because it is one itself. Left to become one, killed a Cyber-Shogun and the army of Cyber-Ninja cunt bastards of fallen dead bodies. A trail of blood behind the Red Beast.

The weapon in question was a gift from many years ago. A female master blacksmith. Ariel Gem who was blind with beauty, skin so smooth and tits like the Goddess Aphrodite. Golden and pale to its liking until he killed her with his cock cannon that she made for him. A mistake that cost him dearly.

Banished from the Cyber-Shogun who lost his one daughter.

Three hundred lashes before he left the Temple's dark oak red double doors of the arena. Hurt and in pain.

Vengeance drove him to kill and now it wants the Death-Heads to die. Why? Because he can and the job pays 600,000 GVA creds.

It growls. "Spit on you stupid Ninja X Fuckers. Now I gotta clean up the mess you made."

The Red Beast hears something close by and sees a flicker of digital camouflage beside a door down the way. Hiding behind the door frame. Half naked with a long rapier.

"Ah, the French man. You don't respect wood do you?" he asked.

The camouflage disengages and the full bronze skin of the French man appears.

He glides his rapier across the arm sharpening the blade on its nanotech purple arms.

"Bonjour, I see we are looking for a certain famous couple."

"Where are they now?" The Red Beast asked.

"I'd tell you, my friend," the French man said.

"You don't even sound French?"

"Yeah, I get that alot. I just like to pretend I'm intimidating," he said.

"Wearing that leather codpiece says it all."

"You turned on." He smiled.

"Not a snow fucking balls chance in hell!" The Red Beast roared.

The French man raised his hand in protest and nodded, apologizing.

"Seems to me we have a kill order to end this for good."

The Red Beast moves swiftly into the elevator.

"We will see about that, combatant," he mumbled.

He hits the button. "You coming or what?"

The French man hits a button on his arm and a trench coat forms out of his shoulders wrapping his half naked body.

"That's better," he said.

They appear through the club's entrance on the twentieth floor and see the place vacant of life, but the sound of music is blaring immensely.

The Red Beast sees a pile of fucked up Cyberpunkies naked and mutilated.

The French man walks up next to his large sized body and stands slanted with his hands on his rapier sword hilt. "Wow, that's what I call an Orgy massacre."

"This is the handy work of the Ninja X Fuckers. A mess and sloppy too," The Red Beast said.

The French man hears something and takes a look behind the spinning sound turntables on the stage and walks up the step.

"Hmmm, look what we have here."

The Red Beast sniffs and approaches near him, overshadowing his height.

He looks curiously seeing a naked woman with purple hair with a tatted sculpted body. Smeared eyeliner on her white face.

She sees them and fears what comes next.

The French man approaches her cautiously with his hands up.

"I'm gonna untie you, Mon Cherie."

"Careful with her, she could be packing hidden weapons and working for the Ninjas," the Red Beast said to him.

Moments later...

The purple haired woman is in black sequin pants and a white tank top supplied by one of the dead female Cyberpunkies.

-The French man hand picked it according to her body frame.
Perfection he said.-

"What's your story?"

The Beast leans slowly up on the wall behind the stage near the exit door.

"We are here to hunt and what about you?" he asked her, staring at her lustfully. Her tits are perfect and round making him feel stiff.

She sits on the stage stretching her neck and her bust rises by inhaling the musky air and exhales out.

"Probably should tell you I'm just a victim and was hurt by those fucking Ninjas trying to rape me, but fought them off until one of them knocked me out cold. I think they just jerked off on my body and left their mark," she said.

"What's your name, luv?"

She looked at the French man's lean frame and touched her neck slowly feeling the sexual arousal inside her. "Sarah BBX at your service."

The French man offers her a hand and she takes it being lifted on two feet. She smirks at him and he winks at her.

The Red Beast scoffs and hands her a handgun. "Ever used one of these?" He asked.

She nodded and cocks back the slide and checks the bullet and clip.

"Impressive. A woman after my own heart," the Red Beast said.

She sticks it in her back and walks off to the exit door. "Are we going or what?"

The French man hits the Red Beast in the arm with a light punch and he notices.

"Yeah, never do that again, friend," he said.

"Ah, come on. Ain't no arm or foul here. Just fun." the French man laughed.

-The Beast follows her out the door and looks back at him. Grins wide. Muthafuck has no clue what she is.-

6. Get the fuckers by the balls!

Devermando fires off two shots into the Ninja X Fucker and rips it's balls out. He continues as the ladies are spread out in other places of the maze.

He turns a corner to the right, sees one standing by the wall camouflaged and thinks it doesn't see him.

He takes his fist punching it through the wall of a blue neon lit room with a couple fucking on a trapezoid sculpture made for sacrificing.

The woman screams as she gets pounded so hard by the Cyberpunkie with an uncircumcised white cock in her wet hole.

He grabs the enemy by the top of the hooded mask and sticks his fingers in its eyes and pulls them out with bloody wires attached to optics inside the skull and it vanishes into smoke like a ghost. "Well that's fucking new."

The Cyberpunkie couple fucking stops and the guy has something in his hand. A glint of metal. A blade for killing.

The guy's brown acne face looks right at Devermando and he sees the black paint across the Cyberpunkie eyes.

Devermando knows what's coming next. The Cyberpunkie killer runs at him with the blade and Devermando grabs him by the throat with brute force.

Snaps his arm in two.

The blade drops on the floor. Pinging noise erupts from the knife hitting the metal tiles.

"Ain't no way I'd let you kill her if it wasn't for me crashing your party. No lady as pretty as her deserves death."

Devermando throws him across the room. CRASHING! The tinted windows break with the Cyberpunkie killer flying through the air and down to his death. But not so.

The killer's body slams into a Cyber-Copter's blades. His limbs tear apart from his body in bloody fashion.

The lady is fully nude, has a texture of purple skin all over her body, she gets up off the statue, walks towards Devermando and grabs his cock inside his suit. "Let me return the favor."

Devermando grabs her by the hair and picks her up in the air against the wall of shadows and she moans screaming of lust. Getting pounded hard by his shaft inside her wet purple meat.

****

Kenzie-Ho and Molly XXX find themselves standing in a room of four walls and three headless Ninja X Fuckers covered in blood on the floor.

They notice the walls have holes in two sides across from each other. They open up revealing brown thick cocks with decent mushroom size tips on the end of them.

They look at each other and giggle, grabbing, ripping each other's clothes off while stroking the cocks with their soft hands.

"These monsters are so big to fit inside my wet pussy," Molly XXX said, moaning, twisting her lips and biting her big natural pale boob. Sucking on her nipple hard. She feels the girth expand inside her and gasps pounding the semen covered brown cock hard coming multiple times. "Fuck me, don't stop."

Her eyes roll back feeling the shaft hit all the way through inside.

The Blond babe watches on and she turns to face the other brown cock in front of her. Deep throating it until it explodes the white cum in her mouth. It splashes all her big fake tits with hot pink nipples. She keeps going at it for a while and finally licks the shaft from the balls and up to the tip.

"These meats are so hard and stiff for us. It's like having your own 24/7 cock to play with."

The action ends when the girls see them disappear back into the walls. They throw their gear back on and slap each other's flabby tush to a job well done.

They go looking for Devermando in the maze's end, Kenzie-Ho stops and senses something behind them.

"We got three figures on our tail."

Molly XXX looks back too and notices one of them.

"That fucking Red Beast. You ain't getting me muthafucka!" she screamed at them.

They pace it quicker through the steel maze that turns circulating right in a spiral towards a doorway.

"What in tarnation is that thing?" Kenzie-Ho asked.

"Not sure babe. It looks like an exit to someplace," Molly XXX said.

The babes keep on inching closer while the baddies behind catch up. Suddenly, two Ninja X Fuckers in white armor pop out of the walls. "It's a trap!"

Kenzie-Ho fires bullets from her Beretta at one of them and it dodges slicing her bullets in half.

"Fuck! Useless."

The sound of crashing through the walls behind the Ninja X Fuckers appears a man the size of a rhino in silhouette and his eyes brighten with rage.

"Devermando!"

Molly sees him grab one of the Ninja's by the head.

7. (Chinese accent) "Yeah, Fuck yo sister!" Middle finger in the air.

He crushes it to bloody bits...
...The other Ninja pulls his blue laser sword from his back and slices Devermando's arm. He sees the cut split wide showing the wires within the bicep.

It hears the sound of someone whistling and feels the rim of an MP7 against its temple.

"You're dead," Molly XXX said.

The sound of the blast pops the Ninja's head blowing it up on the other end.

Devermando sniffs the air and her. "You girls smell like sex."

"I'd say the same about you," she replied to him by grabbing his package.

Kenzie-Ho runs up to the doorway opening and summons them to run to her. "Come on, if you want to make it outta this alive!"

She sees the three mysterious hunters after them. A shot is fired and hits her in the shoulder barely. "Fuck. I'm going in."

-Molly XXX, my love ran in through the door with Kenzie-Ho as I slowly walked backwards firing my shotgun that's always been by my side. I lay some lead down on these muthafucks chasing us. And in that moment I got sucked into the other side. I felt the raw power of a cock cannon firing a laser bullet into my chest. At least that's what I thought it was. Not too sure entirely. But gross I say.-

The blood spills out of Devermando's chest on the black organic skinned floor. He feels the texture. "Where the fuck am I?"

He hears the sound of dark voices screaming in horror. His head turns to the side barely seeing well in the dark with his eyes. Blurry. But his adrenaline is kicking in.

"The fuck is that thing hanging on the wall?"

Molly XXX tits are getting pulled away by black evil hands trying to get a feel of hard nipples.

"Devermando, help me?"

She cries out like a young girl.

Her face begins to change of a horned woman laughing at him as she gets raped by the hands fingering her all over her body parts.

Devermando gasps seeing the fingers transform into black chrome cocks. Green nano-bugs scurrying around them.

The thick veiny girth of the chrome cocks going inside through her fleshy nipples and she has tentacles wrapped around her neck sizzling of acid tearing her bluish pale skin.

"The fucking fuck, did we walk into."

-Nightmares a voice called out. The void of darkness made for pain and agony. Our Damnation!-

Devermando sees her rise in the black void, a white light thrums repeatedly of intense loud sounds hitting his mind and he bleeds out of his nose screaming of pain trying to run away.

The sound of roars comes to life of gigantic monsters called Seeders. Spiked nano-worms pulsing and squirting jizz out of their skinless texture of black blood. Their metal teeth are so grotesque it would make your skin tear without being touched. Mind fucked they say to no end.

Devermando sees the door he went through with such a dark essence of ethereality pulsing around as the three enemies behind that doorway pound fiercely trying to break in.

He hears more voices of hissing and growls coming his way as he paced through the dark of flesh feeling skin throughout the pathway.

He sweats from his neck down feeling the fear hit his mind of the evil beings trying to grab him in a perverse way. Almost raping him.

His neck gets wrapped around with slime neon green tentacles while squeezing it tight until he can't breath.

The sound of gunshots go off and the orange color with hints of bright yellow fire blasting in the darkness. He sees who it is feeling the tentacles retreat from the bullets. The monsters scream and step away into the dark close to the mother of them all.

"Jesus took you long enough to find me," he said.

Kenzie-Ho's body is cut with scraps and bruises of hand prints. She grabs Devermando by the arm. She fires again at the monsters.

"Fucking die muthafucks! Molly should be up ahead waiting for us."

Devermando and Kenzie-Ho run for their lives crossing a gray bridge with light shining at the other end of this madness. She sees the Seeders gain up on them and pushes him through the light.

"Go! I'll be right behind you."

Devermando falls through and ends up on the floor with Molly XXX looking right at him from above.

"Having fun, are we?" she asked.

"I wouldn't exactly call whatever the fuck that was back there fun," he said.

He gets up seeing his weapons and grabs it. "What was that place?"

Molly XXX has a rocket launcher in hand over her shoulder.

"Cyber Hell of some kind, not sure how it came about."

"Well, I know for certain I'm not gonna fall for traps like that anymore," Devermando said with a chuckle.

Molly XXX sees the door's portal form a person coming through firing her guns while suspended in the air.

"Fucking blast them all to fuck shit now!" Kenzie-Ho screamed.

Molly XXX does just that and the Seeder worm's heads pop out of the portal and she fires a shot off.

"Time to say bye-bye, bitches."

The rocket splits into two mini nano rockets that hit the Seeders through the neck and they scream a foul sound that makes everyone cover their ears.

They dissolve into black liquid that digitally dissolves back into the portal like slime. "Goddamn that was loud," he said.

"Come on, let's have ourselves a fucking party," Kenzie-Ho said.

"When you say party, you mean fucking right?" Molly XXX asked.

She winks at her and slaps her right on Molly XXX cute tushy butt.

"Absolutely lover girl."

The Giants of Cyber Bang City stroll pass the black buildings and the Death-Heads along with their fuck toy disappear into the wind.

A second later…

Three silhouettes stand on top of roof access with sun setting behind them.

"We lost them." The Red Beast sneers of hate.

"Perhaps, another time to kill 'em," the French man said.

The Red Beast rubs his gun cock around his pants. "Failure to complete the bounty order is not what I had in mind," he said.

"Not to worry, lover boys, we will get them next time. But perhaps we can service one another at a night club of your choosing,"

Sarah BBX said. Adjusting her large tits and flipping her purple hair. Her eyes turn dark with voices inside her. The monsters control her from the outside to do their bidding. The French man will die soon enough, but the Red Beast suspects them. They will turn him into one of them soon. Or die trying. His power might beat 'em.-

The Red Beast's eyes glare at her and knows what he must do to kill it.

"Let the sodomy begin."

8. Wetworks

///Entry: -Wetworks:
A VR program designed to maximize the inhibitors of the inner flesh providing sexual arousal from the wires attached to the pleasure organs of the human body.-Unknown

The chrome blue lit VR visors across the faces of the three Death-Heads stimulate their minds and Kenzie-Ho draws Devermando's hand down to her wet pussy.

He finger bangs her and she moans as Molly XXX sucks on Devermando's cock up and down feeling the thickness with her sultry plump purple lips like a freaky bitch. Slowly holding her mouth down and gagging on it and her saliva secretes out of her mouth down his shaft. She spits on it. Licking the tip. And giggles. She proceeds again.

The Wetworks program inside their mind is stimulating their brains with a drug called God Mode that enhances their bodies inner nerves creating a kind of numbness.

"Oh that's good babe, fuck you can suck me off good."

Molly XXX backs off the cock and jumps on the bed sideways and grabs his cock sticking it inside her beat pussy. "That's it baby, fuck me now. I want that cock sensation ravishing me apart."

Kenzie-Ho chimes in on the Virtual world inside her visor and sees a video accessing it. -Dark and mysterious she thought.-

The file opens with a black haired Cyber-Geisha violating herself with a cybercock machine. Wearing nothing but spiked metal cups on her tits.

Kenzie-Ho raises a brow and likes what she sees. She feels Devermando hand

finger her as she screams, moaning coming to a climax. The video glitches of green lines skipping.
"The fuck?"

She sees it...
...The white eyes move slowly as a huge silhouette in the green mist grabs the Cyber-Geisha by the neck ripping it off her shoulders. The blood gushed out of her where the neck used to be.

Finally, it slowly moves with long horns coming out into the white light above.

Revealing a Cyber-Samurai with a grotesque naked body of faces pressing out of the skin like they are trapped.

She throws the visor off her face and watches it slam on the ground with the video still running.

The Cyber-Samurai beast snarls, eating the flesh of the twitching Cyber-Geisha and the white eyes look at Kenzie-Ho.

The sound of roaring laughter scares the Death-Heads out of the visors making them stop fucking.
"What the hell is that thing?" Molly XXX asked.
"No clue, but whatever it is it can't be good. And I'm not sticking around to find out," Kenzie-Ho said.

They both look at each other and the visor shuts off. Kenzie-Ho puts her clothes on over her hot revealing body zipping up the crack of her massive tits.
"See ya around."

Devermando jumps out at her and grabs Kenzie-Ho by the arm and she lets go of it, walking out the dark apartment door revealing the chaos of Cyber Bang City on fire.
"Shit. We gotta hit the road, babe."

Seeing the flames burning one of purple Giants leaning limp on a black building that has been destroyed. The orange and red fire burns in his eyes.

He sees the Demon Drones and Cyber-Copter fly by them.

///Entry: -The Island City burns. The rise of Valkyrian is coming.- Unknown

///End Transmission///

The Death-Heads will return.

About the Author

Born 1980 in Northern California and moved to Orange County where I was raised most of my life. I have been writing for 15 years now and enjoy every minute of it. I'm a huge fan of science fiction, cyberpunk, anime, and manga.

To my fans, please spread the word out to friends, people you talk to and on social media about my stories. I would really appreciate it if you rate and leave an honest review.

Thank you,

Carter Holland

www.ingramcontent.com/pod-product-compliance
Lightning Source LLC
LaVergne TN
LVHW031607060526
838201LV00063B/4766